# WHAT DOES A DEFENSIVE BACK DO?

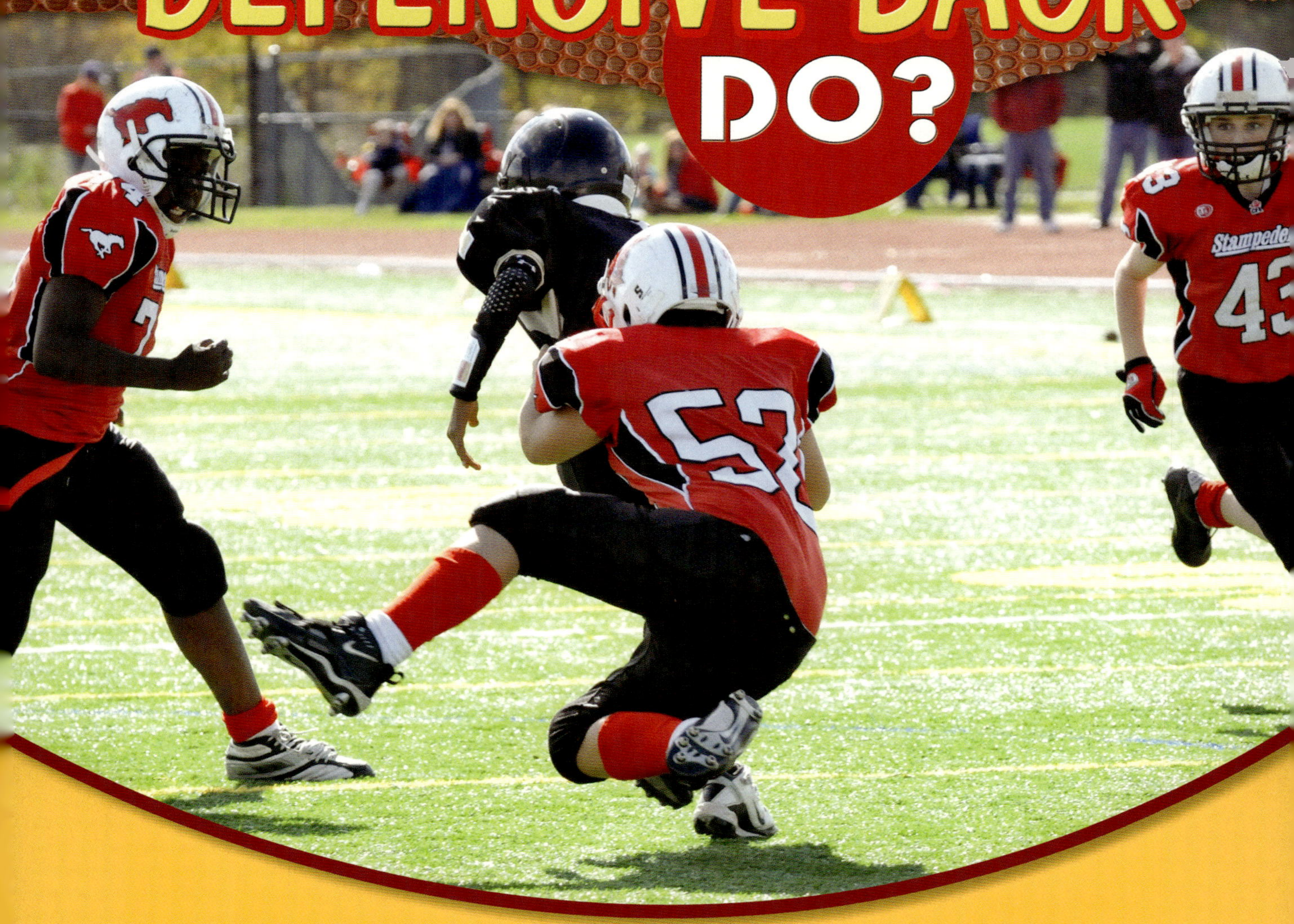


Paul Challen

PowerKiDS press
New York

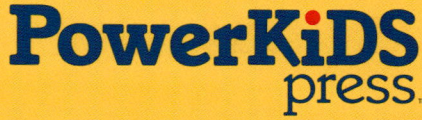

Published in 2015 by The Rosen Publishing Group, Inc.
29 East 21st Street, New York, NY 10010

Copyright © 2015 by The Rosen Publishing Group, Inc.

All rights reserved. No part of this book may be reproduced in any form without permission in writing from the publisher, except by a reviewer.

Produced for Rosen by BlueApple*Works* Inc.
Art Director: Tibor Choleva
Designer: Joshua Avramson
Photo Research: Jane Reid
Editor for BlueApple*Works*: Melissa McClellan
US Editor: Joshua Shadowens

Photo Credits: Cover, p. 9 Susan Leggett/Shutterstock; p. 1, 6, 8, 10, 12, 16, 17, 18, 19, 21, 22 Andy Cruz; p. 3 Alhovik/Shutterstock, background Bruno Ferrari/Shutterstock; p. 4 Dennis Ku/Shutterstock; p. 5, 14 James Boardman/Dreamstime; p. 7 Lawrence Weslowski Jr/Dreamstime; p. 11 Action Sports Photography/Shutterstock; p. 13 Richard Paul Kane/Shutterstock; p. 15 Alan Crosthwaite/Dreamstime; p. 20 Eric Broder Van Dyke/Shutterstock; p. 23 Aspen Photo/Shutterstock; p. 24 Americanspirit/Dreamstime; p. 25 Melinda Dove/Dreamstime; p. 26 left, 27 top Jerry Coli/Dreamstime; p. 26 right Rick Sargeant/Dreamstime; p. 27 bottom Goldnelk/Dreamstime; p. 28 Kenneth D Durden/Dreamstime; p. 29 Peter Weber/Shutterstock

Publisher's Cataloging Data

Challen, Paul.
What does a defensive back do? / by Paul Challen.
p. cm. — (Football smarts)
Includes index.
ISBN 978-1-4777-6990-4 (library binding) — ISBN 978-1-4777-6991-1 (pbk.) — ISBN 978-1-4777-6992-8 (6-pack)
1. Defensive backs (Football) — United States — Juvenile literature. 2. Football — United States — Juvenile literature. I. Challen, Paul C. (Paul Clarence), 1967–. II. Title.
GV951.18 C43 2015
796.332—d23

Manufactured in the United States of America

CPSIA Compliance Information: Batch #WS14PK8 For Further Information contact: Rosen Publishing, New York, New York at 1-800-237-9932

# TABLE OF CONTENTS

| | |
|---|---|
| The Football Team | 4 |
| Strategy | 6 |
| Coverage | 8 |
| In the Zone | 10 |
| The Right Stance | 12 |
| Pass Defenders | 14 |
| Footwork | 16 |
| Bump and Run | 18 |
| Defending Zones | 20 |
| Playing the Run | 22 |
| The Role of a Coach | 24 |
| The Best Defensive Backs | 26 |
| Be a Good Sport | 28 |
| Glossary | 30 |
| For More Information | 31 |
| Index | 32 |

# THE FOOTBALL TEAM

The offensive and defensive sides of a football team have very different jobs to do—but both are crucial to a team's success. At all levels of the game, a balanced attack and a solid **defense** combine to win games. Many different skills are needed to be a good football player on both **offense** and defense.

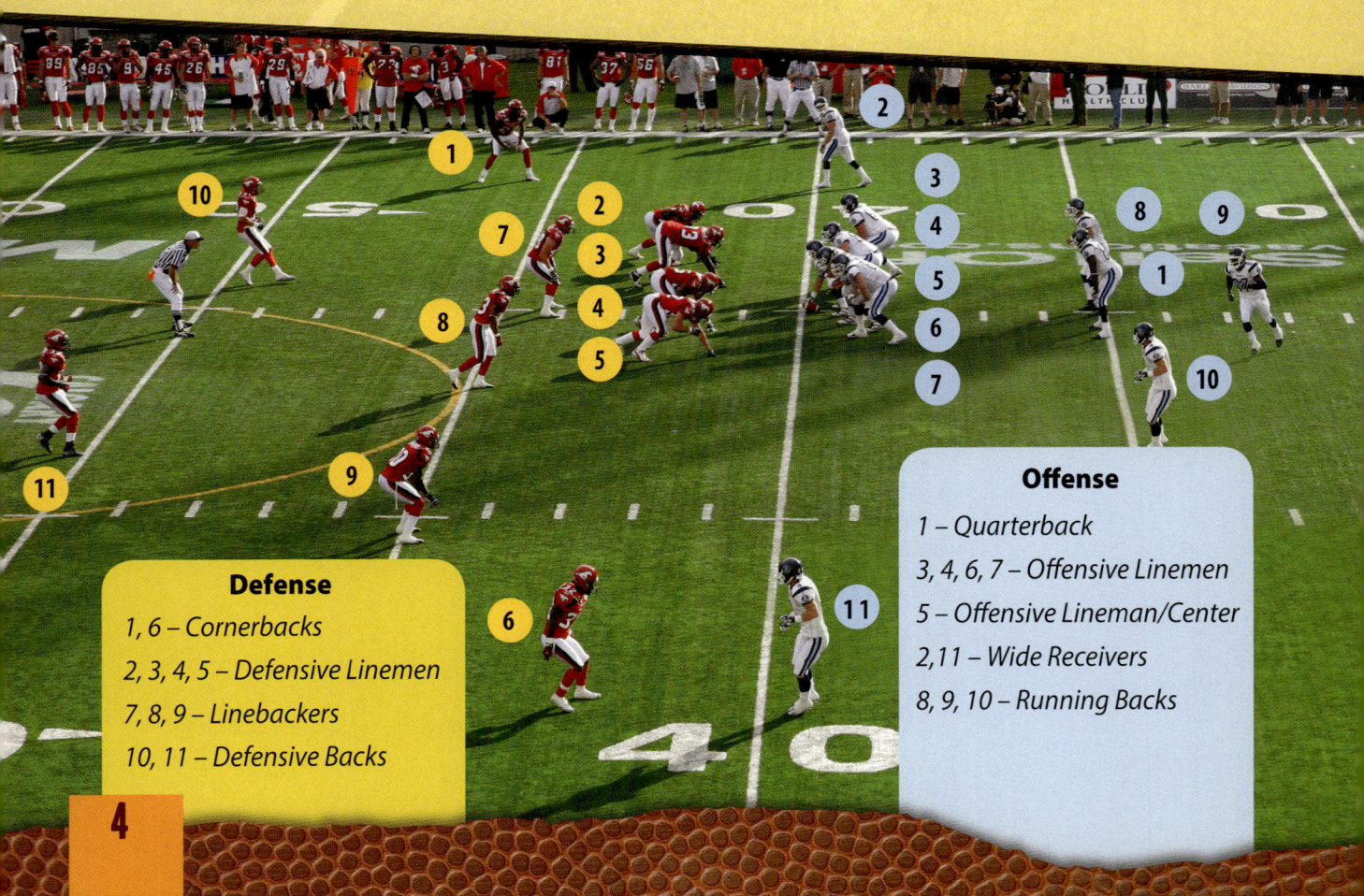

**Defense**
1, 6 – Cornerbacks
2, 3, 4, 5 – Defensive Linemen
7, 8, 9 – Linebackers
10, 11 – Defensive Backs

**Offense**
1 – Quarterback
3, 4, 6, 7 – Offensive Linemen
5 – Offensive Lineman/Center
2, 11 – Wide Receivers
8, 9, 10 – Running Backs

Defensive players try to keep the **opponents** from scoring points. A team's defense is made up of linemen who start each play at the **line of scrimmage** facing the opponent's offensive line. Behind them are the linebackers, and backing them up is the defensive secondary, made up of safeties and cornerbacks. The common name for the players in the secondary is defensive back.

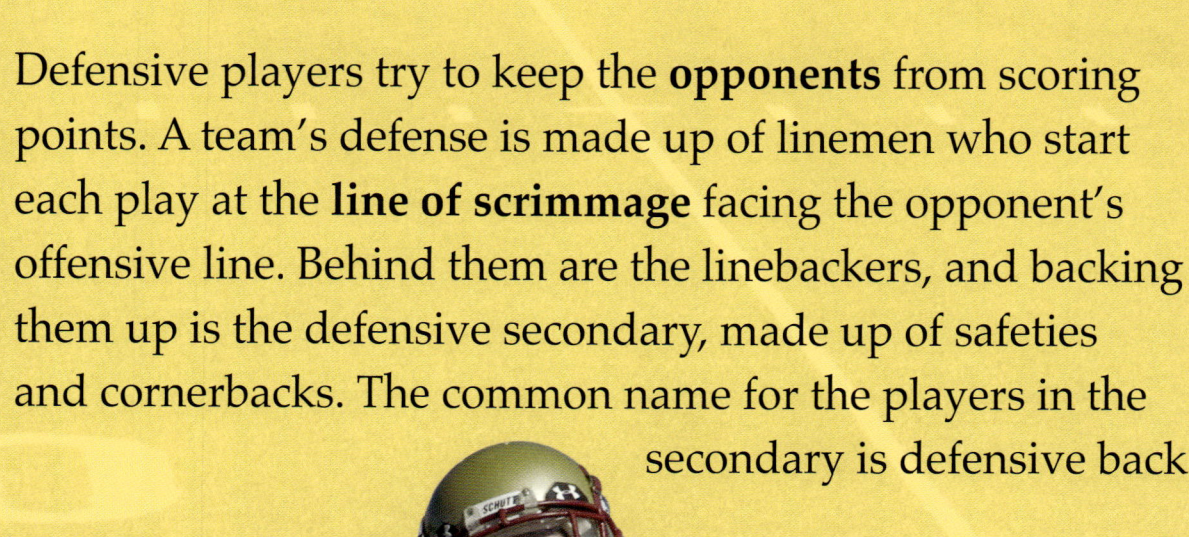

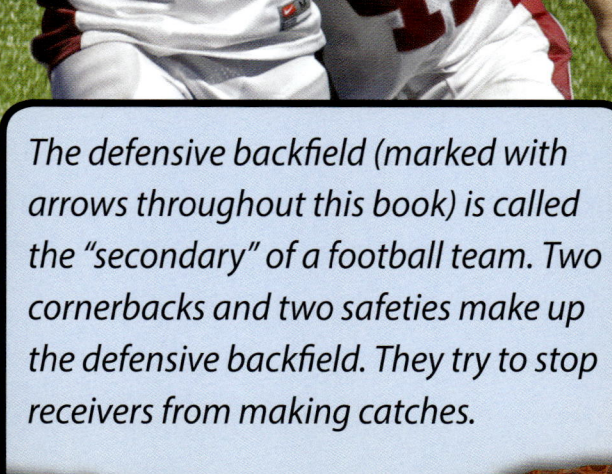

The defensive backfield (marked with arrows throughout this book) is called the "secondary" of a football team. Two cornerbacks and two safeties make up the defensive backfield. They try to stop receivers from making catches.

5

## STRATEGY

When a football team has the ball, the offense must move it down the field using running or passing plays, and attempt to score a **touchdown** or kick a **field goal**. The defense tries to stop them. Both sides face off at the line of scrimmage on each play in a game.

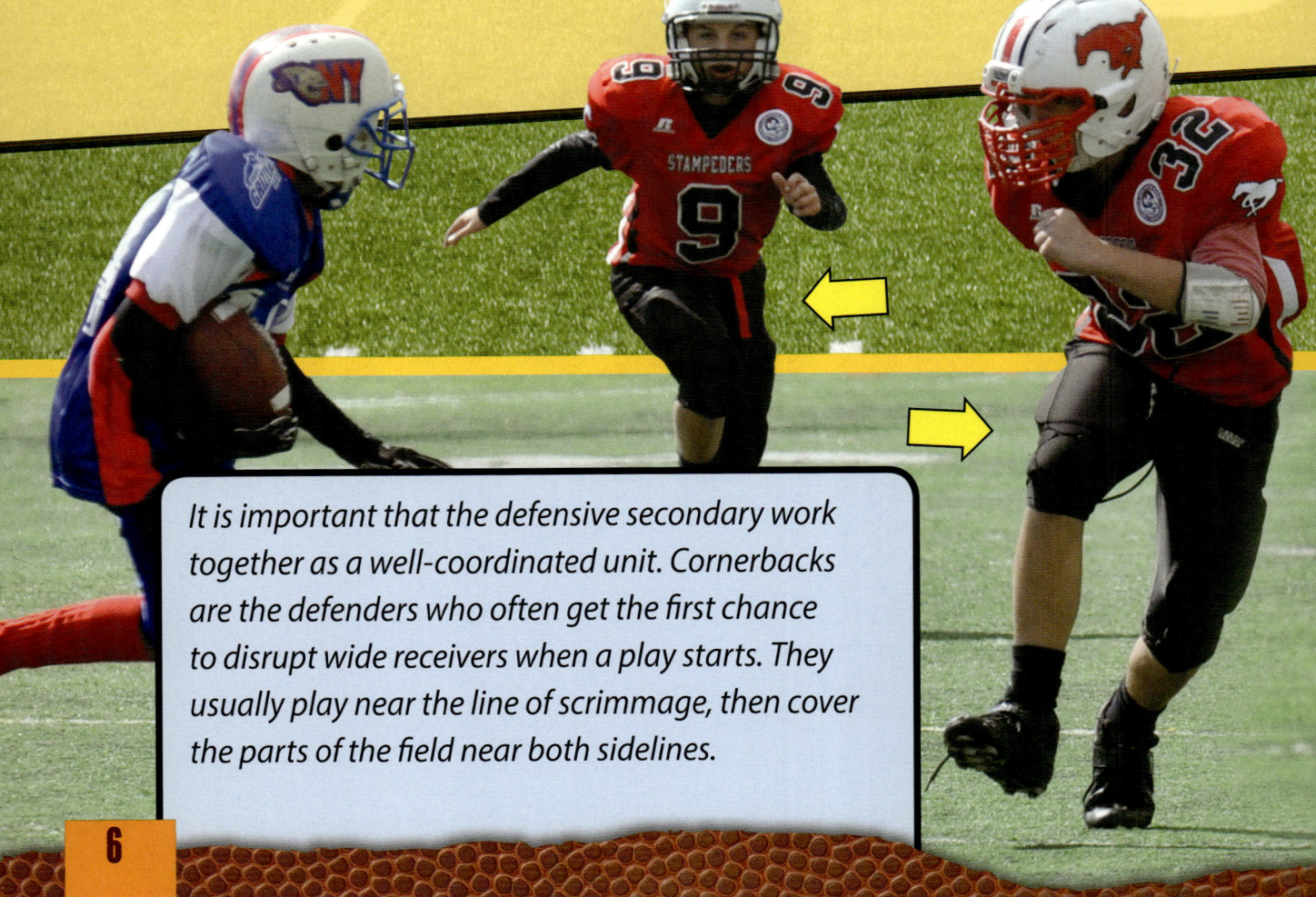

It is important that the defensive secondary work together as a well-coordinated unit. Cornerbacks are the defenders who often get the first chance to disrupt wide receivers when a play starts. They usually play near the line of scrimmage, then cover the parts of the field near both sidelines.

The defense is the team that begins a play without having the football. Defensive players try to keep the other team from advancing the ball and scoring points. They try to tackle ball carriers and prevent receivers from catching the ball.

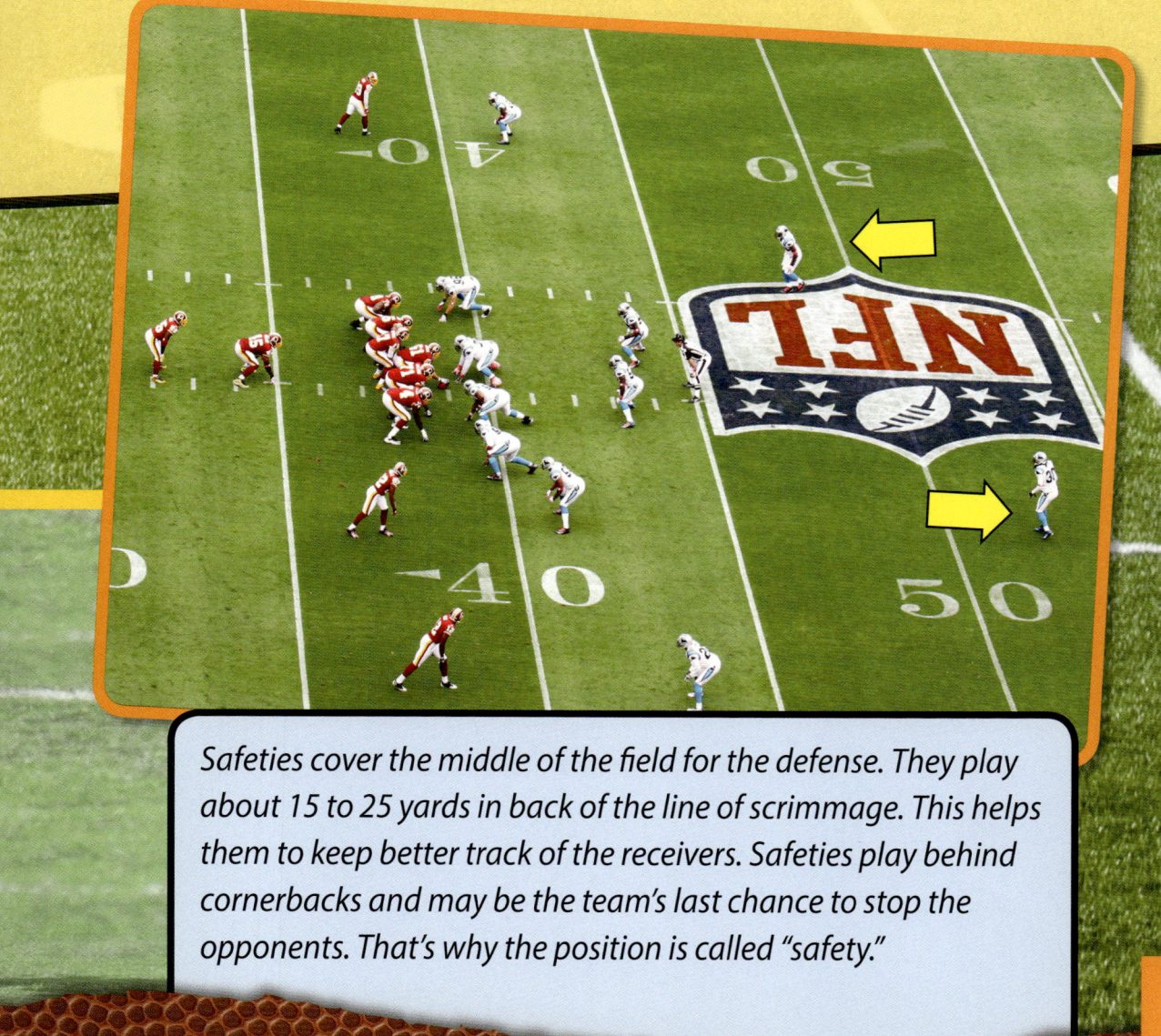

*Safeties cover the middle of the field for the defense. They play about 15 to 25 yards in back of the line of scrimmage. This helps them to keep better track of the receivers. Safeties play behind cornerbacks and may be the team's last chance to stop the opponents. That's why the position is called "safety."*

# COVERAGE

When the ball is snapped, the defensive backs need to position themselves on the field in the best possible spots to stop passes from being completed. This is known in football as pass coverage. Although pass coverage has many combinations, there are only two basic kinds of coverage a defensive back can use: man-to-man and zone.

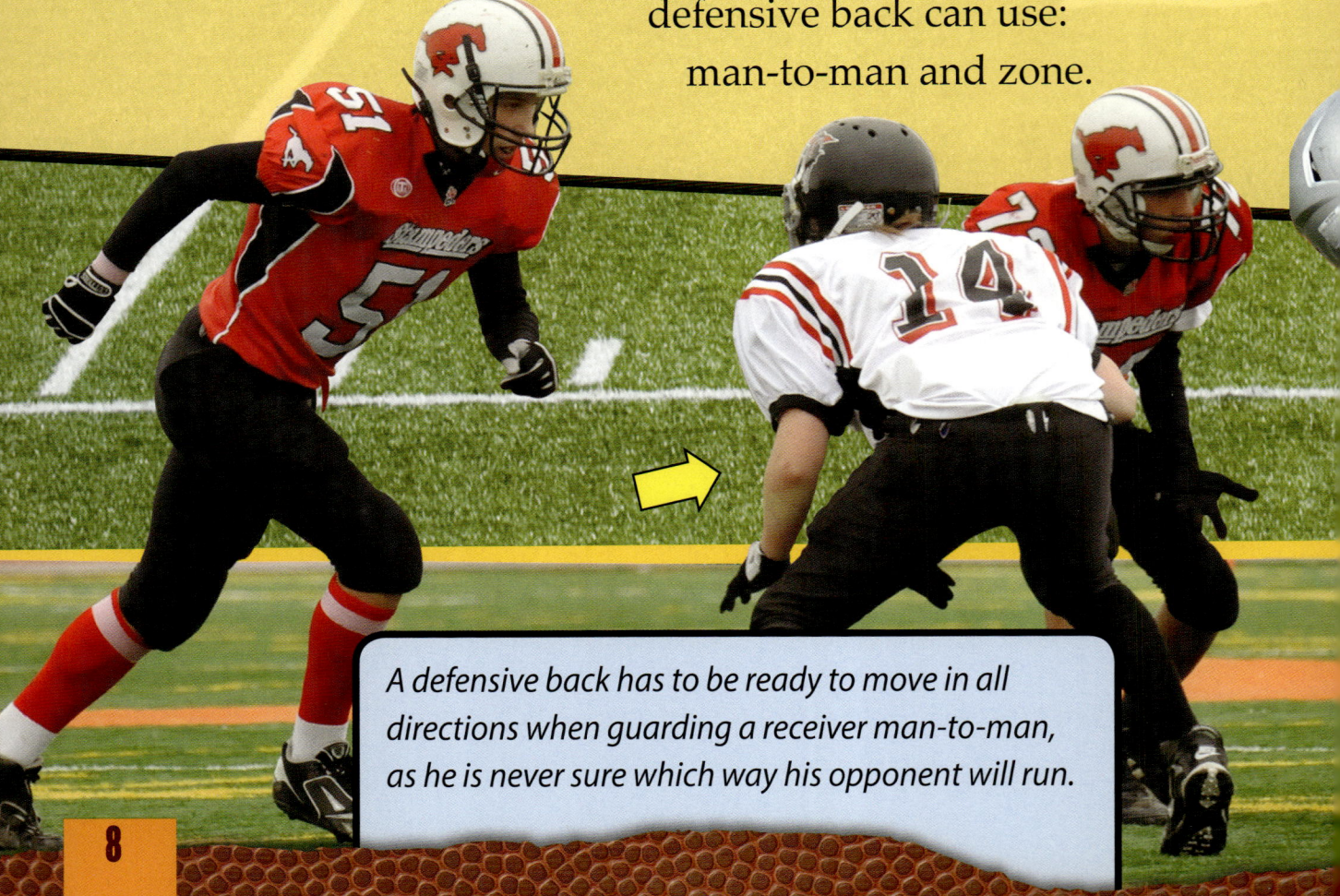

A defensive back has to be ready to move in all directions when guarding a receiver man-to-man, as he is never sure which way his opponent will run.

## DID YOU KNOW?

Cornerbacks are usually the team's fastest defensive backs. They must be agile as well as speedy. NFL teams look for cornerbacks who can run the 40-yard dash in 4.4 seconds, weigh 180 to 190 pounds, and stand 6 feet (1.8 m) tall or taller. Many pro cornerbacks today are not 6-footers, but their average height is growing. They need to be taller because the wide receivers are getting taller, too.

In man-to-man coverage, a defensive back sticks with his receiver as the offensive player runs downfield. The defender covers his assigned receiver wherever he goes until the play ends. He is allowed to bump the receiver near the line of scrimmage but cannot **interfere** with him while he runs his pass route.

Defensive players try to prevent a pass completion by staying close to their assigned receivers. They must be careful not to cause interference.

# IN THE ZONE

In zone coverage, defensive backs work as a unit to cover areas, or zones, of the field. The defense tries to sense what the offense is planning to do. When a receiver comes into a defensive back's zone, the defender becomes responsible for covering the receiver.

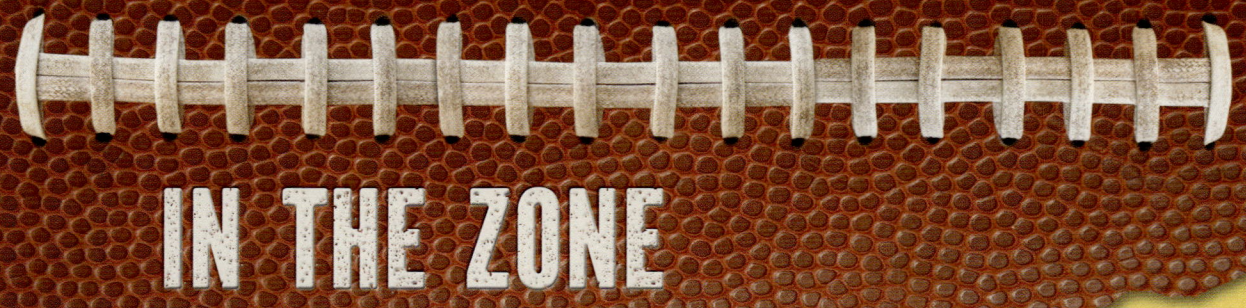

*Zone coverage can often lead to two defensive backs covering the same receiver—good odds for the defense!*

Safeties often specialize in zone coverage, as they take up positions in the middle of the field, far back from the line of scrimmage. Defensive backs keep an eye on receivers in their area, but they must concentrate on the quarterback so they can react to his arm motion and the flight of the ball. When receivers come into their zones, they try to knock the ball away, intercept it, or tackle a receiver who has made a catch.

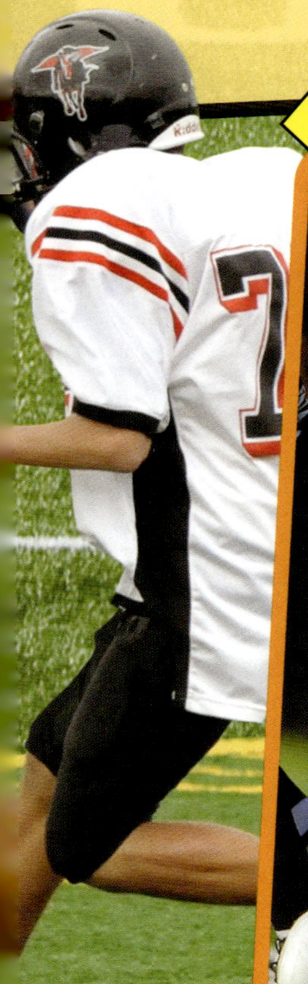

*A defensive back's job is to stop the opposing team from gaining yards.*

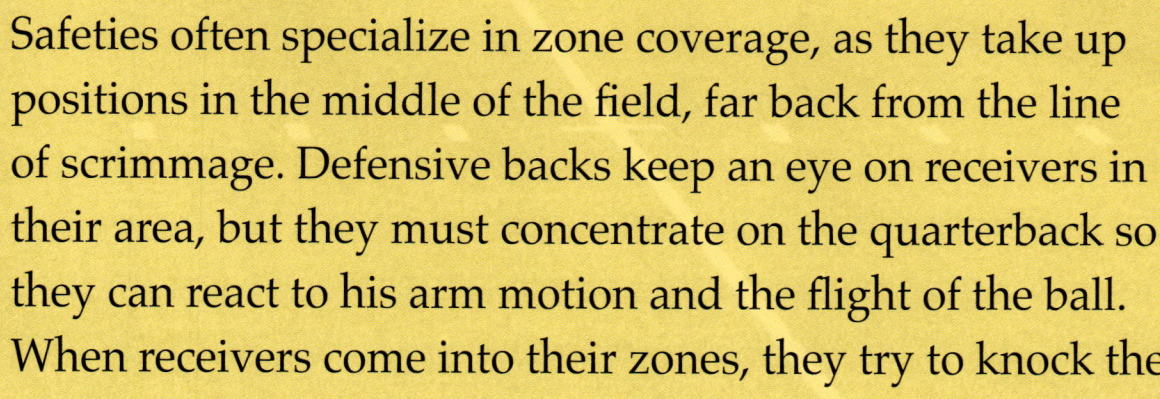

# THE RIGHT STANCE

It is very important that defensive backs position themselves in the right **stance** to start each play. They have to be in a position that allows them to react instantly to plays developing around them, so they drop into a semi-crouch with knees bent and ready to move in any direction. Players at the line of scrimmage use one of three main stances: two-point, three-point, and four-point.

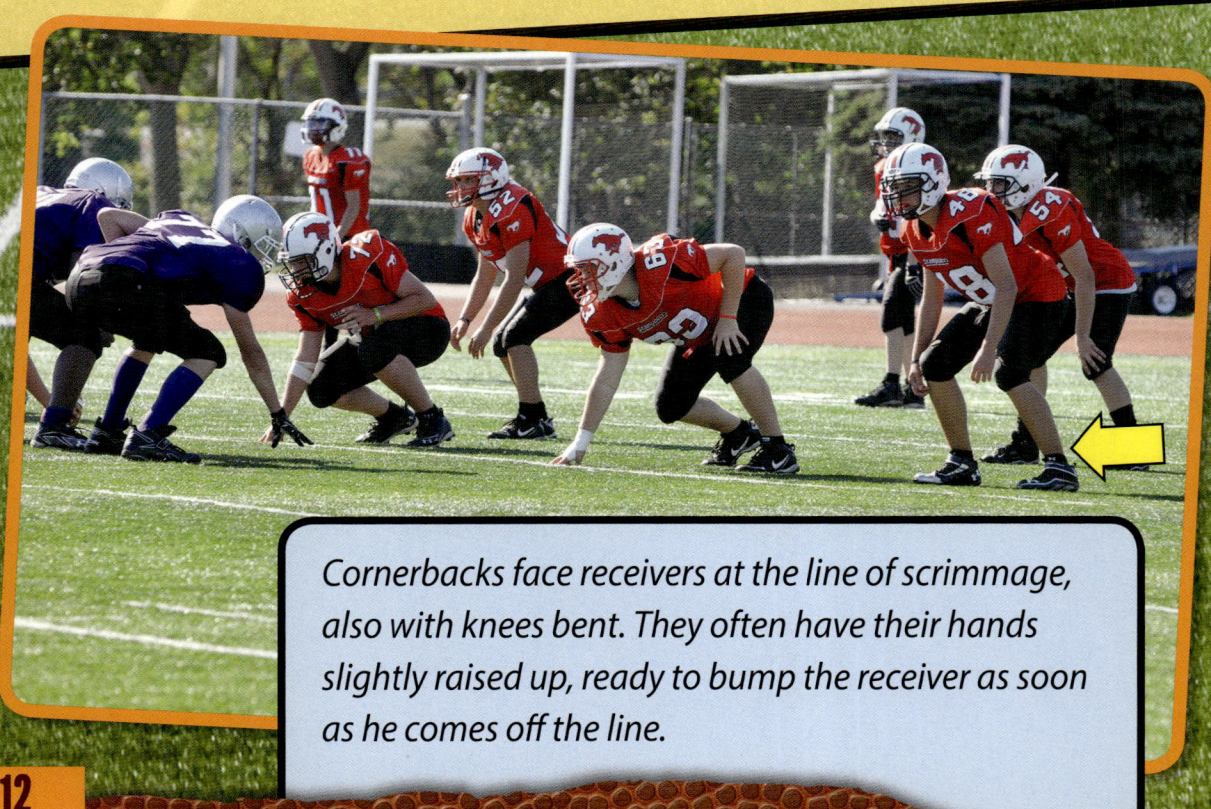

Cornerbacks face receivers at the line of scrimmage, also with knees bent. They often have their hands slightly raised up, ready to bump the receiver as soon as he comes off the line.

The "points" in a stance tell how many times a player's body touches the ground in that stance. In a two-point stance, both feet are touching. This is the simplest stance. It is used when a defensive back needs a clear view in front of him.

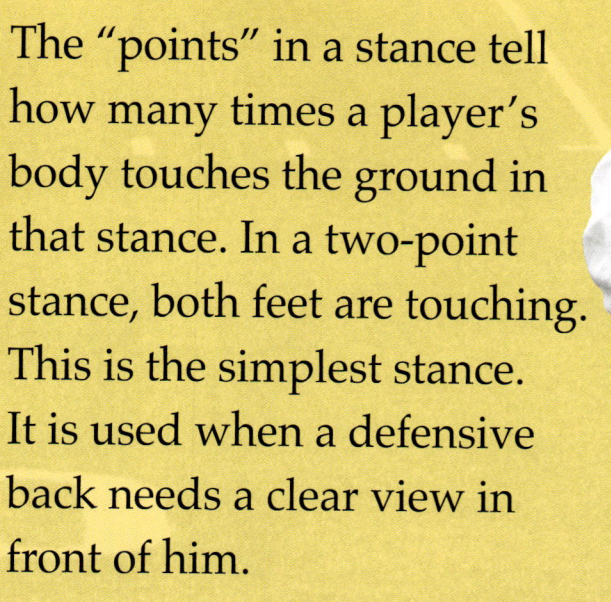

*A defensive back has to be ready to react to a receiver's pass route and must be in the right stance to do that. Often, the first step will need to be backward to keep pace with a speedy receiver.*

# PASS DEFENDERS

Defensive backs need a great sense of timing to play the position well. Not only do they have to stick with fast-running receivers, but they also need to judge the flight of the ball. A pass defender tries to keep the ball away from receivers or to intercept it by catching it himself.

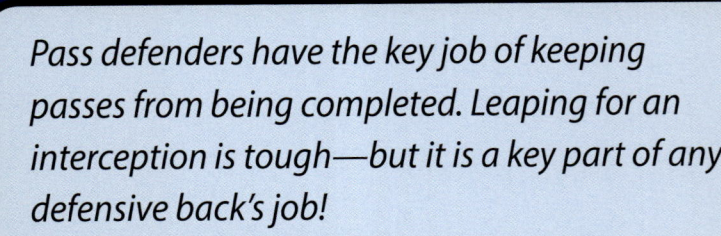

Pass defenders have the key job of keeping passes from being completed. Leaping for an interception is tough—but it is a key part of any defensive back's job!

### DID YOU KNOW?

The Pittsburgh Steelers of the 1970s were one of the best teams in NFL history. Much of their success was because of their great defensive line. The Steelers' defense stopped opposing offenses in their tracks. In 1976, they went on stretch of nine games without allowing a touchdown. A Pittsburgh radio station challenged fans to come up with a name for the team's defense. "Steel Curtain" was the winning name!

When a quarterback releases a pass, should a defensive back step in front of a receiver to try to knock the ball away? Drop back a couple of steps and try to make an **interception** while jumping with the receiver? Or is he arriving too late to stop the pass, and it is a better idea simply to make the tackle if the ball is caught? Defensive backs are constantly having to make such decisions!

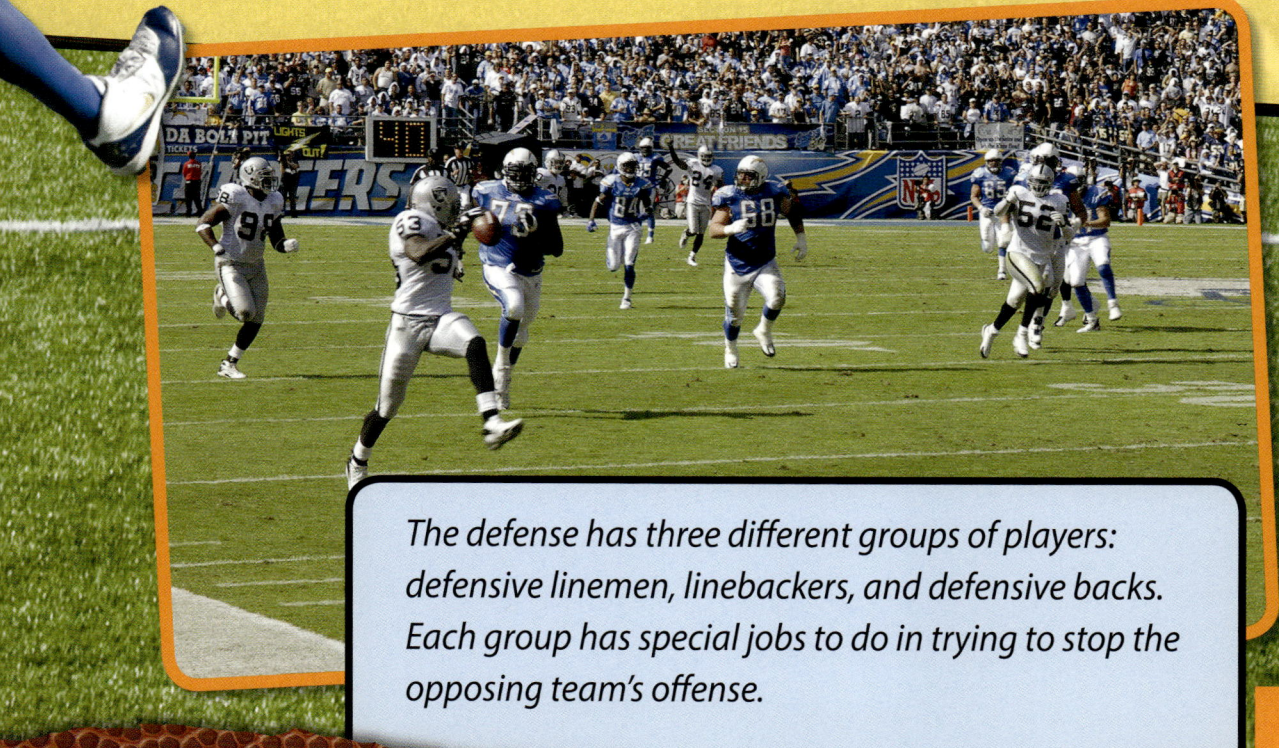

The defense has three different groups of players: defensive linemen, linebackers, and defensive backs. Each group has special jobs to do in trying to stop the opposing team's offense.

15

# FOOTWORK

Defensive backs must have great footwork. To stick with tricky receivers, they must pedal backwards, zip from side to side, and sprint forwards. Quick feet are crucial to play this position well!

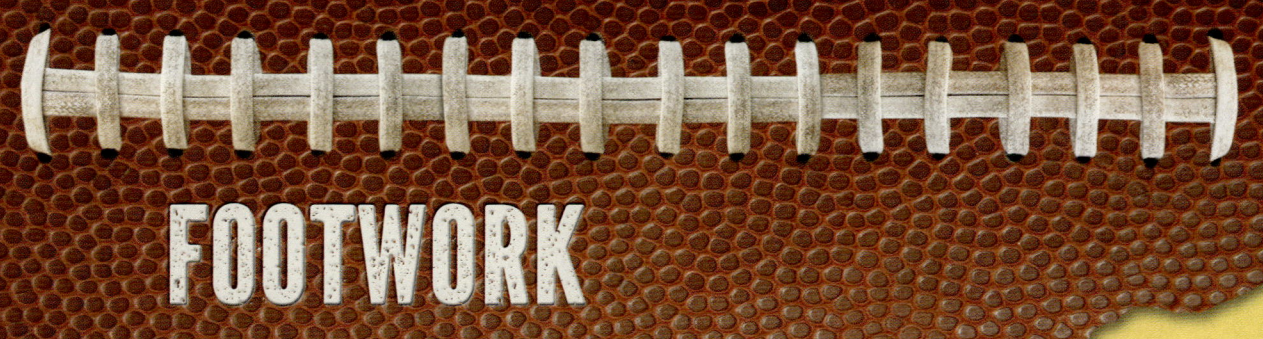

Defensive backs need fast footwork to stay with receivers and ball carriers. Sometimes this means back-pedaling to get in position to make an interception or tackle.

Sometimes to stick with a receiver a defensive back must use a "roll over" run. This means lifting one leg diagonally over the other in a sideways "rolling" motion. It is tough to master this form of running, but it is a very effective way to cover a receiver. Being able to start fast and stop fast is also important because defensive players often must change directions quickly.

*When the ball is in the air, a defensive back cannot tackle or interfere with a receiver. So great footwork skills are important for position.*

# BUMP AND RUN

Depending on whether a cornerback wants to push the receiver out to the sideline, or back into the field of play, he will line up just to the left or right of his opponent. Then at the **snap**, he can give the receiver a bump to push him in the direction he wants.

*A defensive back gets ready to bump a receiver. The bump is used to slow down the receiver and make it more difficult for him to get open. The defensive player tries to make a good bump on the offensive player at the start of a play.*

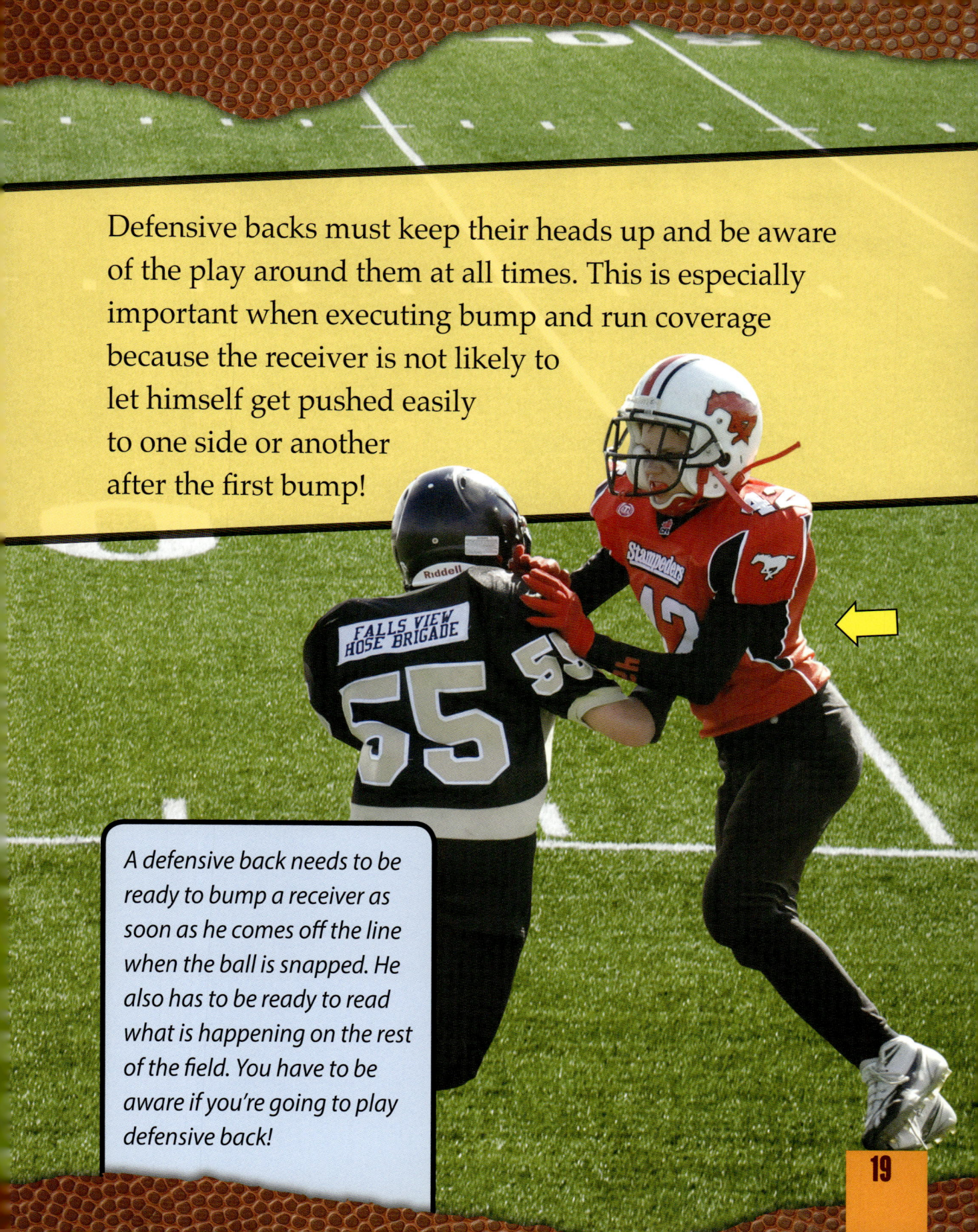

Defensive backs must keep their heads up and be aware of the play around them at all times. This is especially important when executing bump and run coverage because the receiver is not likely to let himself get pushed easily to one side or another after the first bump!

A defensive back needs to be ready to bump a receiver as soon as he comes off the line when the ball is snapped. He also has to be ready to read what is happening on the rest of the field. You have to be aware if you're going to play defensive back!

# DEFENDING ZONES

In a zone defense, linebackers and defensive backs cover specific areas of the field. They try to make it difficult for the opponents to complete a pass. A defensive back needs to understand which zone he is covering, and then carry out that coverage successfully.

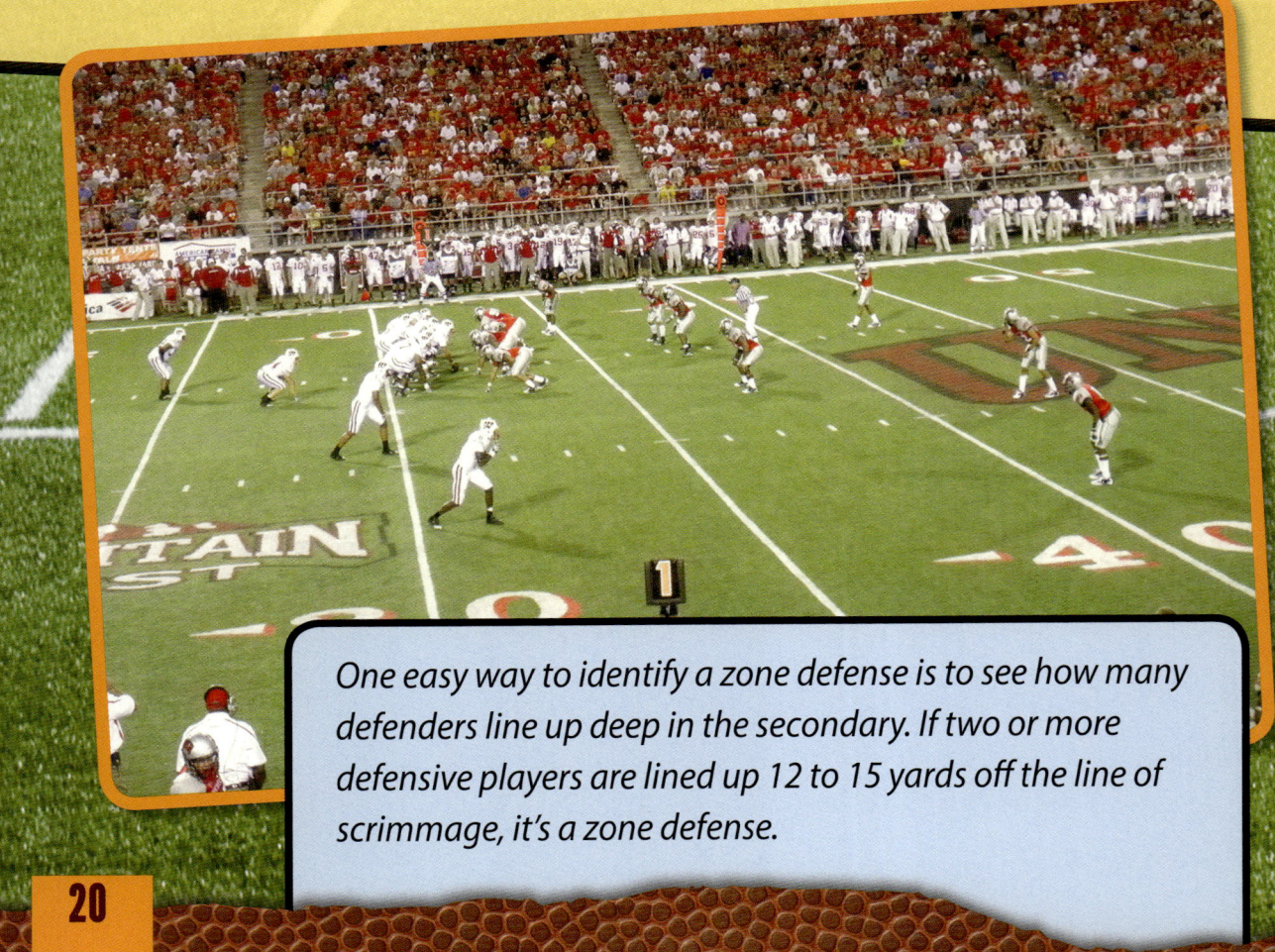

One easy way to identify a zone defense is to see how many defenders line up deep in the secondary. If two or more defensive players are lined up 12 to 15 yards off the line of scrimmage, it's a zone defense.

Before each down, the defensive unit will huddle and plan the next play. It's very important that the defensive backs understand how the defense will execute as a unit, especially when defending in a zone. If everyone does their job, the defensive **backfield** works in harmony with the defensive line and linebackers to shut down any run or pass!

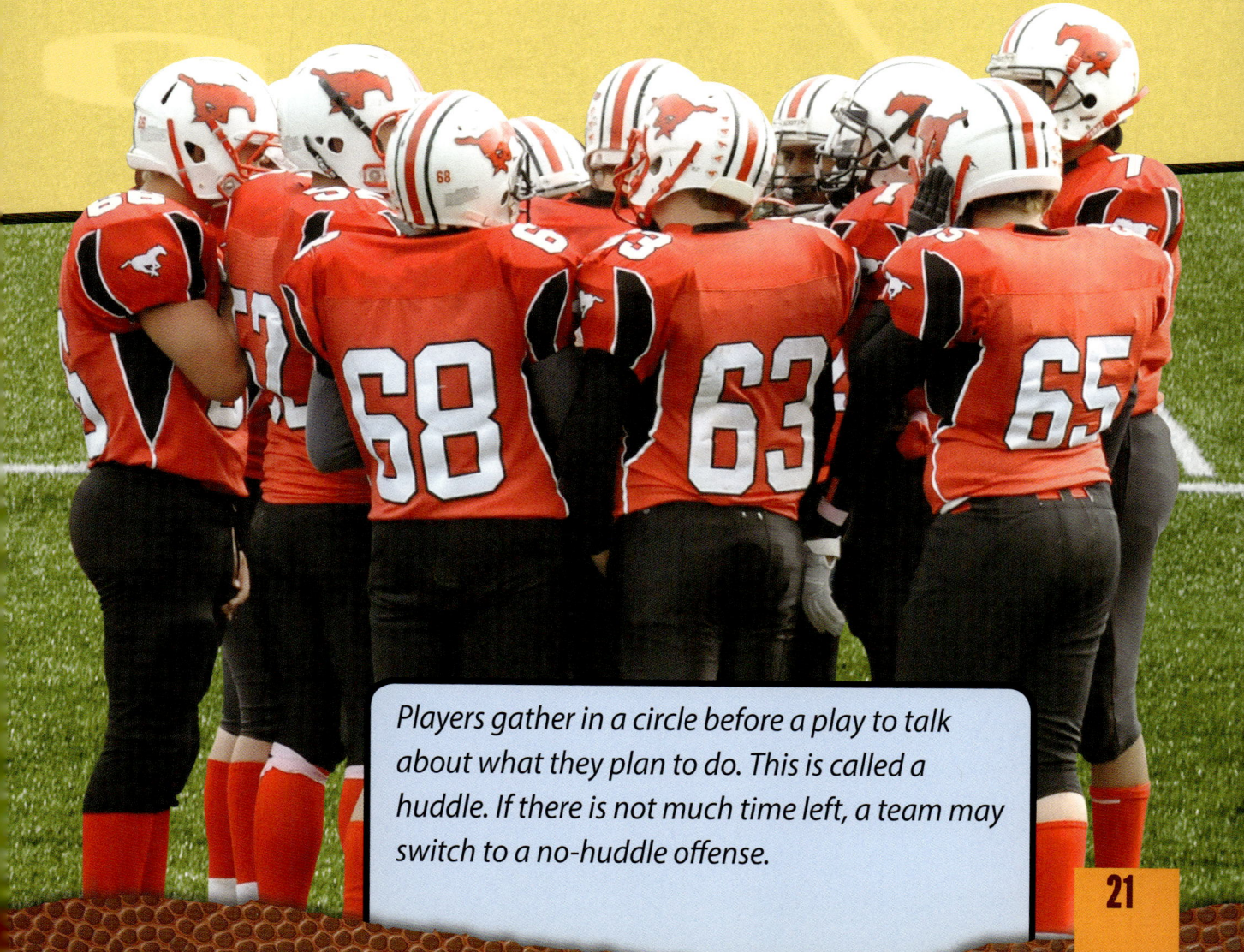

Players gather in a circle before a play to talk about what they plan to do. This is called a huddle. If there is not much time left, a team may switch to a no-huddle offense.

# PLAYING THE RUN

Playing defensive back is not always about stopping the pass. When a ball carrier breaks into the secondary, he must be stopped, and it's often the defensive back who flies in with a tackle! In a tackle, a player makes contact as he tries to stop an opponent, often throwing him to the ground.

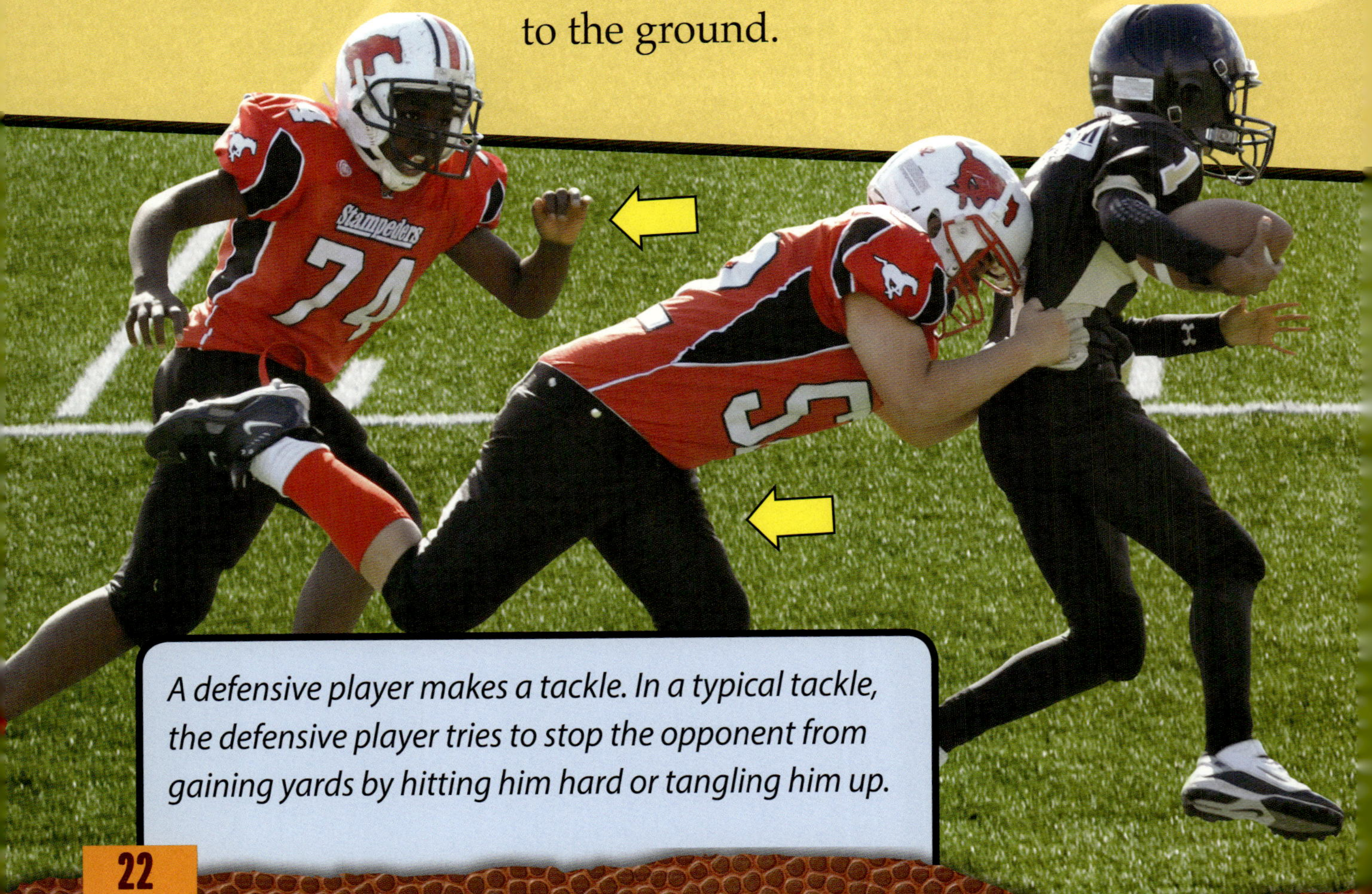

*A defensive player makes a tackle. In a typical tackle, the defensive player tries to stop the opponent from gaining yards by hitting him hard or tangling him up.*

## DID YOU KNOW?

One of the most exciting defensive plays in football is the safety blitz. This happens when a safety leaves his position in the defensive backfield when the ball is snapped and tries to sprint through a hole in the offensive line. He's looking to sack the quarterback or tackle a ball carrier for a loss. Safeties who blitz need to be strong and fearless to execute this play. It's risky, however, because it may open the way for a quick, short pass.

Defensive backs often have the important job of forcing a ball carrier towards the sidelines and out of bounds. This requires a lot of speed because the running back will often try to run wide and then "turn the corner" and head upfield. A fast defensive back can often succeed in forcing the runner to avoid blocks.

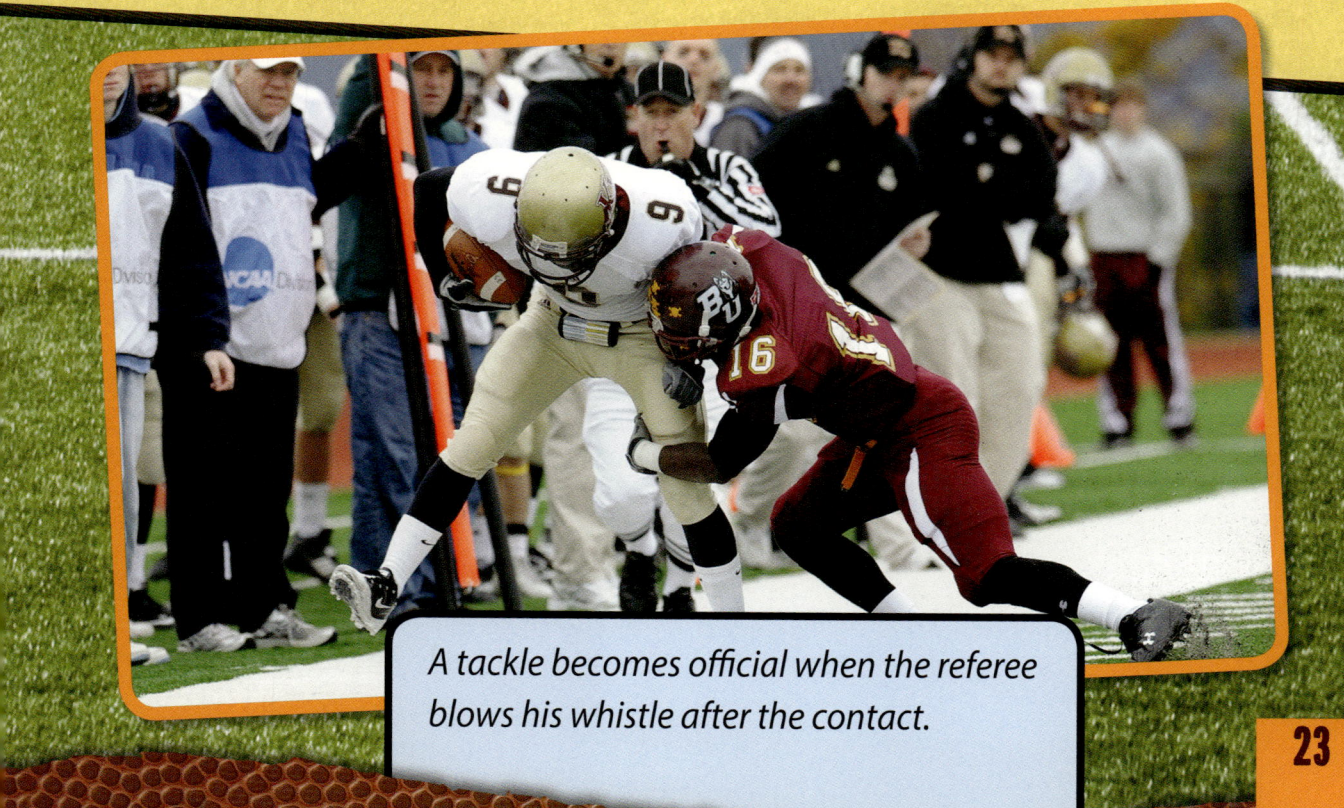

A tackle becomes official when the referee blows his whistle after the contact.

# THE ROLE OF A COACH

Being a head football coach takes a lot of work. You have to be an expert on both offense and defense, as well as on motivating players, running successful practices, and working with an entire coaching staff to make sure your team is prepared for game day.

A good coach helps young players learn to succeed in life and follow their dreams. Many young football players dream of turning pro, but it's not easy. A player must be talented and work hard to succeed.

Coaches need to be good leaders, as players look to them for inspiration and guidance. Many successful players have gone on to be great coaches after their playing careers. Coaches who played in college and the NFL share their experiences with younger players on their teams.

*Jack Del Rio (right) played in the NFL and then became a coach. He was head coach of the Jacksonville Jaguars and now is with the Denver Broncos.*

# THE BEST DEFENSIVE BACKS

There have been many great defensive backs in football history—players who have combined speed, strength, and a fantastic ability to read the games. Willie Brown of the Oakland Raiders, Rod Woodson of the Pittsburgh Steelers, and Darrell Green of the Washington Redskins all had the ability to dominate receivers, and had great success as defensive backs in the NFL.

Ronnie Lott (left), who played for the San Francisco 49ers in the 1980s, is one of the all-time greats at reading defenses. As a rookie, he ran back three interceptions for touchdowns.

Charles "Peanut" Tillman (right) of the Chicago Bears is another famous defender. He often strips the ball away from receivers after they think they have caught a pass.

### DID YOU KNOW?

One of the best defensive backs of all time was Deion "Prime Time" Sanders, who played for five different NFL teams, including the Dallas Cowboys, between 1989 and 2006. As well as being a standout cornerback, Sanders was a kick-return specialist. He also played pro baseball for nine years while he was in the NFL.

In recent years, Charles Woodson of the Green Bay Packers, Ed Reed of the New York Jets, Darrelle Revis of the Tampa Bay Buccaneers, and Jairus Byrd of the Buffalo Bills have all been outstanding defensive backs and big-time fan favorites.

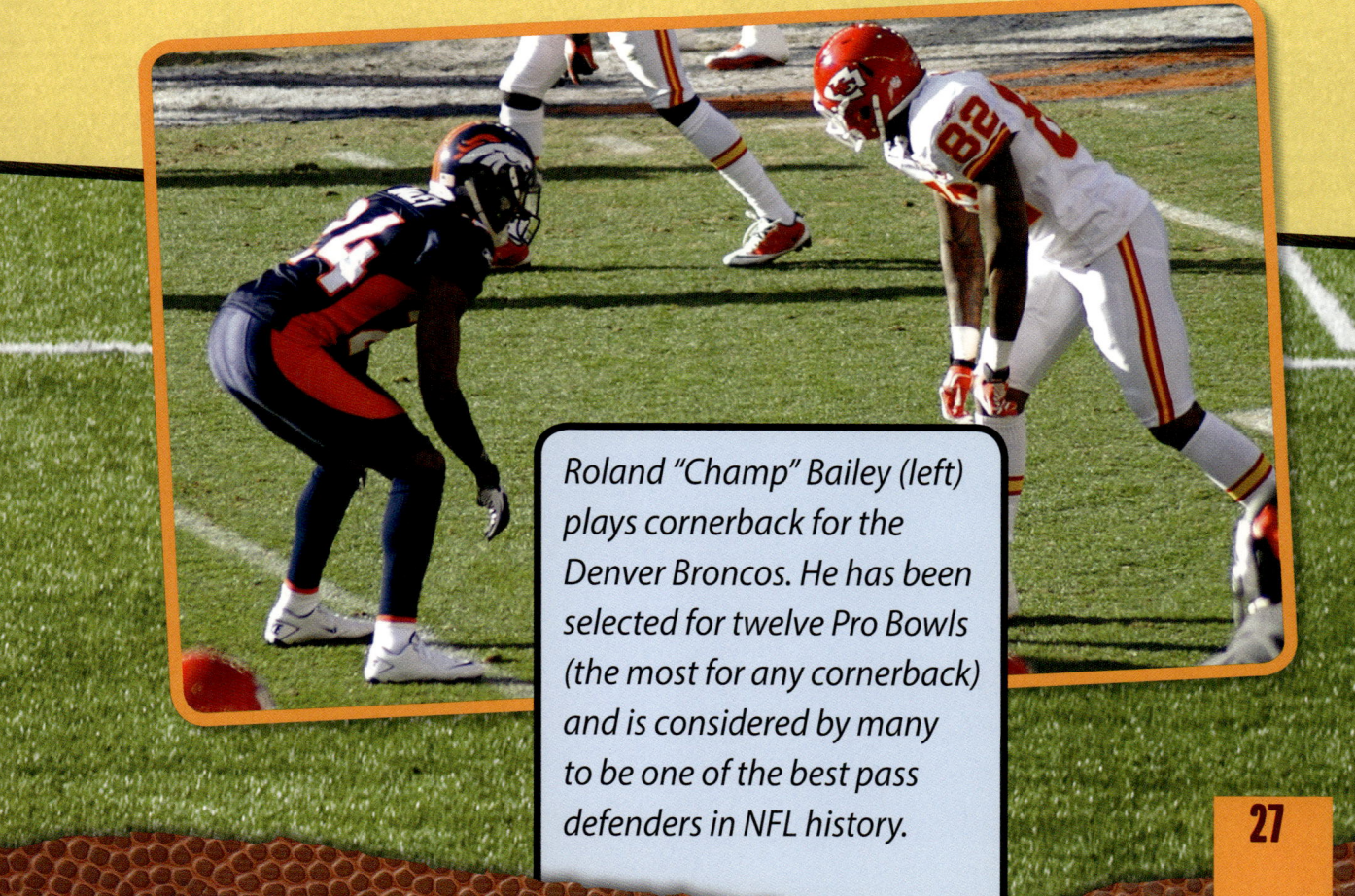

Roland "Champ" Bailey (left) plays cornerback for the Denver Broncos. He has been selected for twelve Pro Bowls (the most for any cornerback) and is considered by many to be one of the best pass defenders in NFL history.

# BE A GOOD SPORT

Being a good sport starts with respect for the game and everyone involved. In the heat of a game—with the fans cheering and both teams trying to win—it is easy to lose your cool and react in a negative way towards the **referees**, your opponents, the fans, and even your coach. That's why it is important to remember that good sportsmanship is a very important part of football.

*It's fine to celebrate when you score a touchdown but good sportsmanship means you don't taunt the other team.*

From youth to the pros, football is played at many age and skill levels. At every level, however, you can see players, coaches, and fans treat one another with respect. They realize that while winning is great, playing a good, fair play is what really matters!

Football is played in all kinds of weather, including rain, snow, and bitter cold. No matter how tough the game gets, teams must play fair! Players should not taunt each other or get so rough that they break the rules. It's also against the rules to yell at the officials or push or hit them.

# GLOSSARY

**backfield** (BAK-feeld) The area behind the line of scrimmage.

**defense** (DEE-fents) A group of players trying to stop points from being scored by the other team.

**field goal** (FEELD GOHL) A play in which the ball is kicked through the uprights of the goalpost.

**interception** (in-ter-SEP-shun) A pass that is caught by the defense.

**interfere** (in-ter-FEER) To get in the way of the receiver so that he does not have a chance to catch the ball.

**line of scrimmage** (LYN UV SKRIH-mij) The invisible line where the ball was last down and where the next play starts.

**offense** (O-fents) A group of players trying to score points for their team.

**opponents** (uh-POH-nents) Another person or team you are competing against in a game.

**referees** (reh-fuh-REEZ) Officials in charge of the game.

**snap** (SNAP) The action of the center tossing the ball between his legs to the quarterback.

**stance** (STANS) A way of standing.

**touchdown** (TUCH-down) A play worth six points when a player carries or catches the ball in their opponents' end zone.

# FOR MORE INFORMATION

## FURTHER READING

Gigliotti, Jim. *Defensive Backs*. Game Day: Football. New York: Gareth Stevens, 2010.

Hurley, Michael. *Football*. Fantastic Sports Facts. Mankato, MN: Capstone Press, 2013.

Mahaney, Ian F. *The Math of Football*. Sports Math. New York: PowerKids Press, 2012.

## WEBSITES

Due to the changing nature of Internet links, PowerKids Press has developed an online list of websites related to the subject of this book. This site is updated regularly. Please use this link to access the list:

www.powerkidslinks.com/fbs/def/

# INDEX

**B**
backfield  5, 21, 23

**C**
cornerbacks  5, 6, 7, 9, 12, 18, 27

**D**
defender  6, 9, 10, 14, 20, 26, 27
defensive secondary  5, 6

**F**
field goal  6
footwork  16, 17

**I**
intercept  11, 14
interception  14, 15, 16, 26

**L**
linebackers  5, 15, 20, 21
linemen  5, 15
line of scrimmage  5, 6, 7, 9, 12, 20

**M**
man-to-man coverage  8, 9

**N**
NFL  9, 15, 25, 26, 27

**O**
offense  6, 10, 15, 21, 24
offensive  4, 5, 9, 18, 23
opponents  5, 7, 8, 18, 20, 22, 28

**P**
pass coverage  8

**Q**
quarterback  11, 15, 23

**R**
receivers  5, 6, 7, 8, 9, 10, 11, 12, 13, 14, 15, 16, 17, 18, 19, 26

**S**
safeties  5, 7, 11, 23
safety blitz  23
snap  18
stance  12, 13

**T**
tackle  7, 11, 15, 16, 17, 22, 23
touchdown  6, 15, 26, 28

**Z**
zone coverage  8, 10, 11

1/28/15